Whose Footprints?

Written by Claire Llewellyn

Look! Here are some footprints.

Who made them?

Footprints

Was it a bird or a cat?

It was a bird.

Bird

A bird's foot looks like this.

Foot

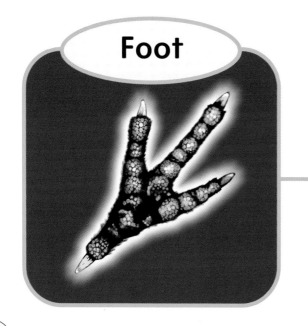

Footprint

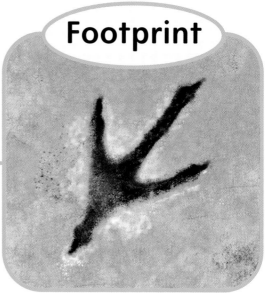

Here are some more footprints.

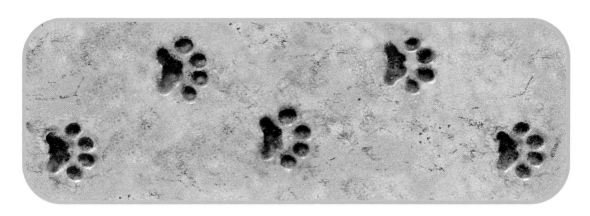

Who made them?

Was it a cat or a cow?

It was a cat.

Cat

A cat's foot looks like this.

Foot

Footprint

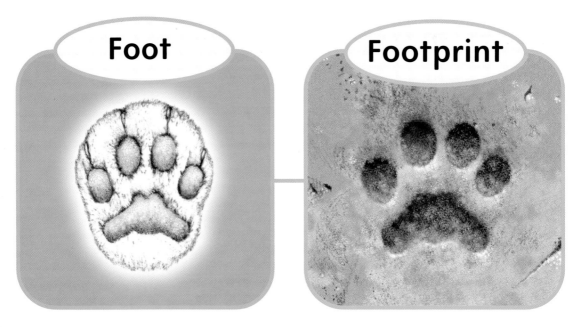

Here are some more footprints.

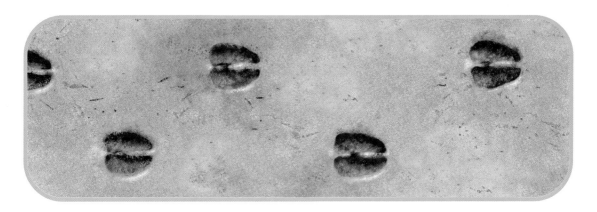

Who made them?

Was it a cow or a dog?

It was a cow.

Cow

A cow's foot looks like this.

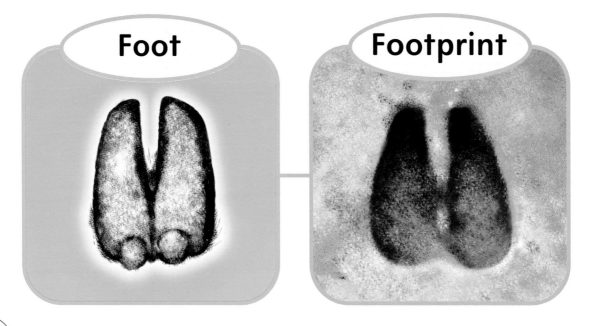

Foot

Footprint

Here are some more footprints.

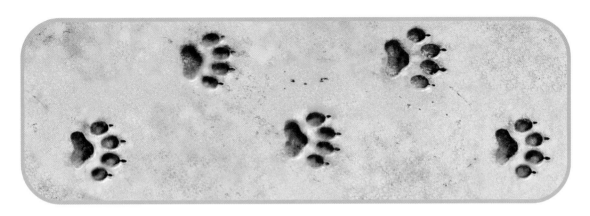

Who made them?

Was it a dog or a rabbit?

It was a dog.

Dog

A dog's foot looks like this.

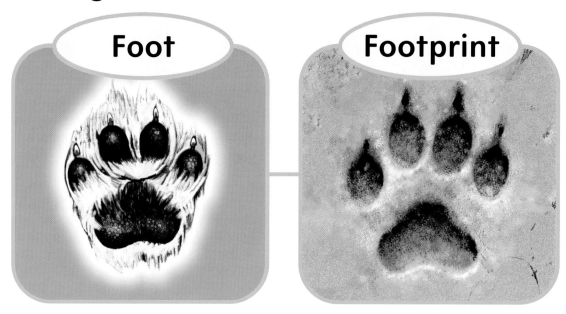

Foot

Footprint

Here are some more footprints.

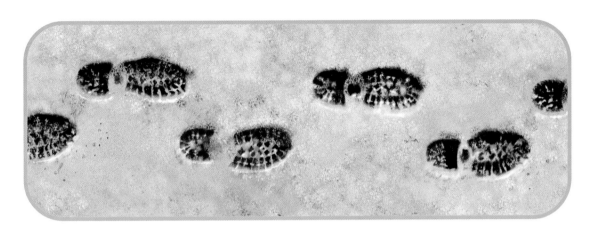

Who made them?

Was it a bird, a cat, a cow, a dog, or a rabbit?

No! It was me!